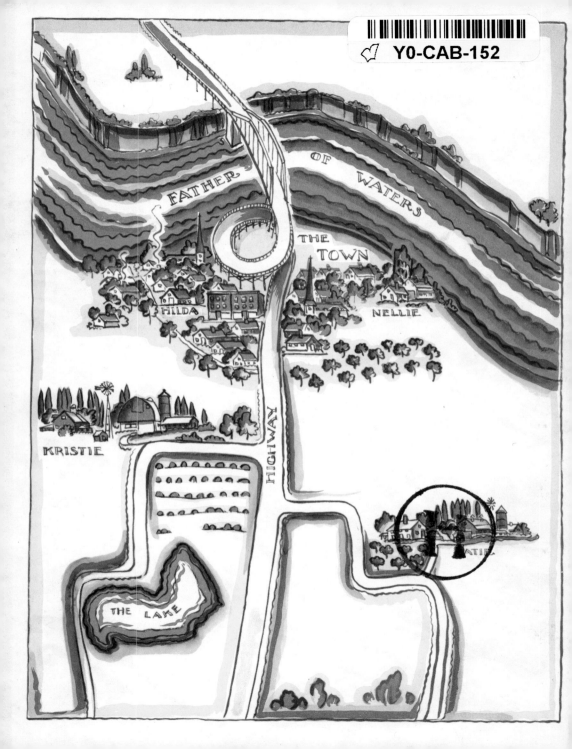

KRISTIE AND THE COLT

AND THE OTHERS

The crackling of fire in a wood stove; the pungent smell of a barn; the simple sounds of ducks and geese; the sloshing of a wooden spoon in rich cake batter; the warm, sweet fragrance of gingerbread baking; the rewarding fun of a happy family project; the love of a boy for an injured gull; the jealousy of an old farm horse for the new young colt —make these simple, down-to-earth stories the kind that children will want to read and read again.

Emma L. Brock

HAS ALSO WRITTEN AND ILLUSTRATED

Skipping Island
Come On-Along, Fish!
Plug-Horse Derby
Ballet for Mary
Kristie Goes to the Fair
Kristie's Buttercup
Three Ring Circus
Surprise Balloon
Little Duchess: Anne of Brittany
The Birds' Christmas Tree
The Umbrella Man
Uncle Bennie Goes Visiting
Mr. Wren's House
The Topsy-Turvy Family
Here Comes Kristie
A Present for Auntie and Too Fast for John
Heedless Susan
Till Potatoes Grow on Trees
The Pig with a Front Porch
Little Fat Gretchen
One Little Indian Boy
The Greedy Goat
To Market! To Market!
The Runaway Sardine

These are BORZOI BOOKS *for Young People*
published by ALFRED A. KNOPF

KRISTIE
AND THE COLT
AND THE OTHERS

written and illustrated by

EMMA L. BROCK

NEW YORK: ALFRED · A · KNOPF

"KRISTIE AND THE COLT" appeared in *Story Parade*, February 1945.

"PEDER'S GULL" appeared in *American Junior Red Cross Journal*, December, 1942.

"TAKING CARE OF NELLIE" appeared in a different version under the title of "WINTER BOARDER" in the February 1947 issue of *Jr.*

For Helen

who asked for another
story about Kristie

Kristie and the Colt—CONTENTS

KRISTIE AND
THE COLT

Elmer and Einer were twins and they were
having a birthday. They were having a birthday and they should have been the happiest
boys in the world. There they sat with the
birthday present between them. Elmer sat on
the left of the present and Einer sat on the
right of it. But their mouths were drooping almost down to their chins.

"Whatever will Kristie say?" whispered
Elmer.

"Yes, what?" Einer whispered back.

Elmer and Einer looked at each other sadly. They petted the present between them.

They looked toward the barn where their good horse Kristie was.

"Whatever will Kristie say?" murmured Elmer.

"She won't like it," said Einer.

"No!" said Elmer and Einer together.

[4]

"If only it had been white like herself," said Elmer, "she might like it better."

"But it's as black as coal, 'cept three of its feet."

Elmer rubbed his hand through his red hair that stood up straight and wiry. Einer pushed back his straw-colored hair that was always in his eyes. Then they petted the present, one, two, one, two. The present liked the petting.

The hired man came out and sat on the fence.

"Well, now," he shouted in a loud and cheerful voice. "What a grand present to have —a colt!"

"Sh-s-sh!" hissed Elmer.

"Kristie doesn't know about it yet. We haven't told her," said Einer.

But Kristie knew something was happening in the barnyard when she heard the voices.

[5]

She whinnied loudly. The little black colt scrambled to its feet and looked around. It was a fine young colt. It had a neat head and a stick tail and legs that were much too long. Kristie whinnied again and the colt galloped off toward the barn.

"Whoa!" cried Elmer.

"Whoa, there!" shouted Einer, and they ran after it.

"Whoa!" called the hired man from the fence rail. "Whoa!"

But the colt did not know what "Whoa" meant and it ran up to the barn door. It leaned forward on its four long legs and whinnied.

"Oh!" cried Elmer as he threw his arms around the colt's neck. "Now Kristie knows."

"Yes, now she knows," said Einer. "Listen to her dance."

He ran into the barn and over to Kristie's stall.

[6]

"Good Old Kristie," he said. "Good Old Kristie."

"We've brought a friend to see you," called Elmer from the door. "A nice friend."

"It has white feet, Kristie," said Einer. "Real white, Kristie."

"You'll like it," called Elmer.

But Kristie kept stepping around and looking over her shoulder. She snorted and blew.

"Bring her out," said Elmer. "I'll hold the colt."

"Good Old Kristie," said Einer. "Come on Kristie. Come on."

Elmer pulled the colt over by the fence. Einer led Kristie to the barn door. She came out with her tail switching and walked over toward the colt.

"Hold out her white feet so Kristie can see them," called Einer.

[7]

But the colt danced away from Elmer. It danced over to Kristie. Elmer held his breath watching Kristie. Einer held his breath too. And the hired man sitting on the fence held his too, waiting to see what Kristie would do.

Kristie nuzzled the colt and snuffed at it. She whiffled and blew big breaths over it. She whinnied and walked all around it. The colt whinnied too and danced until its three white feet glittered in the sun. Elmer and Einer watched with their mouths wide open. What would Kristie do?

Kristie looked at the colt, pushed it with her big white nose and walked away. Elmer and Einer and the colt stared after her. Kristie walked across the barnyard and stood by the gate.

"She doesn't like it," sighed Elmer.

"No, she doesn't like it," sighed Einer. "It's very plain to see that she doesn't like it."

[8]

"Ya, it's yust too bad, but she doesn't like it," said the hired man.

The colt whimpered and lay down and fell asleep.

"Whatever can we do?" asked Elmer.

"We could give the colt away," Einer answered.

"But Dad gave it to us for a birthday present," said Elmer. "We couldn't give it away."

"Well, no. We couldn't."

"Perhaps we could whitewash it," said Elmer.

"I don't think you could whitewash a colt," said Einer, shaking his head.

"Well, maybe not," said Elmer. "Just look at Kristie standing over there."

"Perhaps we could give her some sugar to make her happier," Elmer said.

"But sugar never made Kristie do anything," Elmer answered.

[9]

"Well, no," mumbled Einer.

Elmer and Einer stood there with their hands in their pockets. They looked from Kristie to the colt and from the colt to Kristie. Their mouths were drooping down to their chins.

"We could call her Little Kristie—her, it, the colt, I mean," Elmer said. "Kristie might like that."

"But she'd think we were talking to her," said Einer.

"Well, yes, she might. But we could call her 'K' for short. Little K. How would that be?"

"Sure. Little K. Kristie would like that!" said Einer. "If we could explain it to her."

They looked over at Kristie. She was still standing there by the gate. Her head was hanging and her legs looked more crooked than ever. Elmer and Einer did not try to explain anything to her.

"Poor Old Kristie," sighed Elmer.

"Yes, poor thing. What can we do?"

They sat down beside Little K. and thought and thought.

"Perhaps we could go and ask Axel Peterson. He had Kristie a long time before we bought her from him."

"Yes, he might know what would make Kristie like Little K. We could ask him when we go to town next Saturday night."

Elmer and Einer did not know how they could wait for Saturday night. Five days was so long. But each day they fed Good Old Kristie oats and hay. They rubbed her down and took her out to the pasture every morning. They fed Little K., too, and rubbed her black sides until they shone like shoe blacking. She

[11]

grew fonder and fonder of Elmer and Einer and they liked her, too. They liked her almost as well as they did Kristie.

But Good Old Kristie did not like Little K. a bit. During all those five days she did not look at Little K. once, not once, not even once.

At last, Saturday night came. Elmer and Einer were all dressed up in their best shirts and new overalls. As soon as the supper dishes were washed, Elmer and Einer and their father and their mother and the hired man drove to town in the old green car. Elmer and Einer were in a great hurry to reach Main Street and their father drove as fast as he could. At last, they stopped at the corner drug store. There, as always, was Axel Peterson leaning against the doorpost.

"Hi!" he called. "How is Good Old Kristie?"

"She's fine," said Elmer.

"But she isn't happy," said Einer.

"She doesn't like the colt," they said together.

"The colt?" asked Axel Peterson, his eyes big with surprise.

"The one our father gave us for a birthday present," Elmer said.

"Little Kristie, we call her," said Einer. "Little K. for short."

"Oh, ya?" said Axel, squinting one eye. "So she doesn't like it, the colt, Little K. Yust think of that now!"

"What can we do to make her like her?" asked Elmer and Einer.

"Well, you take care of Kristie all right, do you?" asked Axel, squinting the other eye.

"Oh, yes," said Elmer.

"And we tried sugar lumps, too, to sweeten her up," said Einer.

"Hmm," Axel said, squinting both eyes.

[13]

"Ya, but you pet Little K. a lot, too."

"Oh, yes," said Elmer.

"We're very fond of Little K.," said Einer. "She follows us everywhere."

"Ya, then that's it," said Axel. "Kristie wants to be the only horse. That's yust it."

"Oh," murmured Elmer and Einer. "O-o-o-h."

"Ya, you pay more attention to Kristie. Pet her and play with her and drive her out swimming. Then yust see how yolly she'll be. Then she'll like Little K."

"Oh-h-h!" said Elmer and Einer. "That might do it. Thank you, Mr. Peterson. We'll try that." The corners of their mouths were turned way up.

As soon as they got home, they went into Kristie's stall. They petted her and gave her extra oats to eat. Good Old Kristie.

Every day Elmer and Einer took care of

Kristie. They curried her and brushed her and braided her tail and bangs. They put some fresh shoe blacking on her hat too. It was the hat that had belonged to their mother—the one they had fixed for Kristie when her own hat was eaten by the pigs. Kristie liked that black hat, especially when it smelled strong of blacking. She tossed her head as she took the boys to the lake to go swimming. She looked fat and happy.

Little K. stood around sad and lonesome. She whinnied when she saw Elmer and Einer and she whinnied when she saw Kristie. Of course, Elmer and Einer fed Little K. and they rubbed her down, too, when Kristie was not looking. But the rest of the time they made believe that they did not see Little K. at all.

"Poor K.!" said Elmer.

"She's so unhappy," said Einer.

"Perhaps a week will be long enough to make Kristie like her," Elmer said.

"I hope so," said Einer.

But a week did not do it. Two weeks did not do it. Little K. whinnied and pranced around Kristie. She galloped all around the barnyard, her three white feet glittering in the sun. But Kristie switched her tail and looked the other way.

"Oh, dear," said Elmer. "It isn't going to work."

"No," said Einer. "It is plain to see that it isn't going to work. We must try something else."

"Perhaps we should ask Axel Peterson for another idea," Elmer said. "He knew Kristie a long time before we bought her from him."

"Yes, let's," said Einer. "Tomorrow is Saturday and we'll ask him when we drive into town."

Right after supper that Saturday evening Elmer and Einer and their father and mother and the hired man drove to town in the old green car. They found Axel Peterson leaning against the doorpost of the drug store.

"Hi," he called. "How did it work now?"

"It didn't work," said Elmer.

"She still doesn't like Little K.," said Einer.

"No!" cried Axel in surprise. "Yust think of that now!"

"No, she won't speak to Little K. even," Elmer and Einer said together.

"Hmmmm," muttered Axel Peterson. "Yust think of that! She won't speak to her even."

"No," said Elmer.

"No," said Einer. "What can we do now?"

"Well, let's see. Let's see," said Axel, squinting one eye and then the other and then both together. "Let's see, yust."

Elmer and Einer stared at Axel with their round blue eyes.

"Kristie wears a hat still, doesn't she?" Axel asked.

"Yes, she won't go without a hat," said Elmer.

"Ya, sure," said Axel.

"It's a fine black one that used to belong to our mother," said Einer. "She likes it."

"Mmmmm," said Axel. "Yust so. And Little K. doesn't wear any hat at all?"

"Why, no," said Elmer and Einer together.

"Then that's maybe the trouble," Axel said. "Ya, that's maybe it. Kristie maybe doesn't like a horse without a hat."

"Why, maybe that's it," cried Elmer, looking more cheerful.

"Let's get a hat right away," said Einer.

"Yust try that and Kristie will yolly well like Little K."

"Thank you, Mr. Peterson," and Elmer and Einer ran toward the five-and-ten-cent store. Their mouths were turned way up at the corners.

"I have a dime," said Elmer.

"And I have fifteen cents," said Einer. "A

hat won't cost more than a quarter, not a little horse's hat."

They skipped through the doorway of the five-and-ten-cent store. They dashed up and down the aisles.

"There they are," cried Elmer.

But the hats were all big hats, big hats for farmers and wide hats for gardeners. Much too big for Little K. Their mouths drooped down to their chins. They walked along the aisle.

"What's that?" cried Elmer, pointing.

"It's a sort of hat," said Einer.

"It has a visor in front like a cap," said Elmer, "and it ties behind in a bow."

"Like to see a sun hat?" asked the girl at the counter.

"Oh, it's a sun hat," said Elmer.

"But it's a little hat all right," said Einer.

"We'll take it," said Elmer and Einer together.

"Twenty-five cents," said the girl.

Elmer gave her his ten cents and Einer gave her his fifteen. They were grinning so widely that there was not room for their cheeks between their mouths and their ears. Now Kristie would like Little K. at last! She would like Little K. in the pink hat.

Early next morning as soon as the sun popped up above the horizon, Elmer and Einer ran out to the barn with the pink sun hat.

They led Little K. out into the barnyard. Elmer held her while Einer put on the sun hat. The visor shaded K.'s eyes, the bow was behind her ears and her ears stuck up between. She danced up and down.

"I'll get Kristie," said Elmer.

"I'll hold Little K.," said Einer.

Kristie came out of the barn with her tail switching, but she did not look at Little K.

[21]

"Look, Kristie," called Einer.

"Look, Kristie," cried Elmer. "Look quick."

But Kristie did not look. She went across the barnyard and began eating grass. She did not even glance that way.

Little K. was kicking and biting. She was dancing and bouncing. She galloped over to the fence and began to rub her head against it. She rubbed and rubbed. She kicked up her heels and rubbed. Off came the hat. She stamped on it and jumped on it. It was torn and dirty.

"She doesn't like it," sighed Elmer.

"She won't even wear it," said Einer.

"No, it's plain to see she won't wear it," said Elmer.

"And if she did wear it, Kristie wouldn't look at her to see her wearing it," sighed Einer.

"No," said Elmer.

"No," said Einer, and the corners of their mouths almost met under their chins. What could they do? Whatever could they do to make Kristie like Little K.?

Elmer and Einer thought and thought. They thought all the time they were doing the chores. They thought all the time they were rubbing Kristie down and braiding her tail and her bangs. They thought while they were rubbing down Little K. and washing her white feet. But they did not think of a way to make Good Old Kristie like Little K.

After their work was done, Elmer and Einer sat on the back steps and thought some more. Kristie was nibbling at the grass along the barnyard fence. Little K. was galloping all around. She would gallop up to Kristie and whinny. Every time she did that, Kristie would sneeze and snort through her nose.

"She just sneezes," said Elmer.

"And sneezes," said Einer.

At dinner time the hired man came in from the fields and sat on the fence. And their father came too and began washing up for dinner in the basin beside the door.

"She doesn't like her any better?" he asked, as he scrubbed his face red with the towel.

"No," said Elmer.

"No," said Einer, "not a bit. She just sneezes at her."

"Well," said their father. "At least she sneezes."

"Yes, she sneezes," said Elmer and Einer.

"Good Old Kristie," said their mother in the kitchen doorway. "She's a queer old horse."

"Yes," said Elmer and Einer in one breath.

"Ya," said the hired man. "She's a yolly funny horse."

When they went in to dinner, they left Lit-

tle K. galloping around the barnyard, and Kristie sneezing every time K. came near her.

Elmer and Einer could not eat much dinner. Only a chicken leg or two, and some peas and carrots, and some potatoes, and several baking powder biscuits, and a glass or so of milk. After chocolate cake they went out to sit on the steps and think.

Little K. was running up to Kristie and bumping into her. Good Old Kristie would shift on her crooked legs and sneeze and go on eating.

"Little K. is trying hard to make friends," said Elmer.

"But what good does it do?" murmured Einer.

"Kristie doesn't seem to mind the bumping," said Elmer.

"No," said Einer. "She just sneezes and sneezes," said Einer.

[25]

"I suppose that's better than nothing," Elmer said.

"Well, yes," said Einer.

"Couldn't we do something?" Elmer asked.

"I suppose we could go swimming," said Einer.

"Yes, let's. Kristie needs some exercise. It might help her sneezing."

They pulled the old buggy out from the barn and carried out the harness. They rolled the buggy over to Kristie and they threw the harness on her back. They pulled her ears between the straps and put the bit in her mouth and backed Kristie between the shafts and fastened her to the buggy. Then Elmer and Einer climbed up on the seat.

"Gid-ap," said Elmer, slapping the reins on Kristie's back.

"Gid-ap," said Einer.

Their father was standing by the gate and their mother was on the porch. The hired man was sitting on the fence chewing a grass blade.

"Good-bye," called Elmer.

"Good-bye, Little K.," called Einer.

But Kristie did not move. She stood still and looked over her shoulder.

"Gid-ap, there, Kristie," said Elmer.

"Good Old Kristie," said Einer, but Kristie did not move.

"Whatever is the matter now?" asked Elmer.

"She has on her hat all right," said Einer.

"And Little K. isn't bothering her. She's over in the corner eating grass," said Einer.

"Gid-ap, Kristie!" they both shouted as loud as they could.

But Kristie stood still and stared over her shoulder. Then she danced a little and whinnied loudly. Little K. looked up from her eating. Kristie whinnied loudly again and Little K. came galloping across the barnyard.

Then Kristie stretched out her long thin neck. She stepped out with her four crooked legs and walked quickly across the yard and through the gateway. Little K. came bouncing after her.

"Well, I never!" everybody said. "Well, I never!"

Elmer and Einer were grinning so widely that their pink cheeks almost shut their eyes.

"She spoke to her," whispered Elmer.

"Yes, she did," Einer whispered back.

Kristie stepped along the road, looking over her shoulder to be sure that Little K. was following. Whenever Little K. stopped to nibble grass, Kristie whinnied softly and Little K. would follow along.

Elmer and Einer did not say another word. They were waiting to see what Kristie would

do next. They came to the road on the left that led to the schoolhouse. Kristie turned left as she always did at every road, but Little K. ran straight on. Good Old Kristie looked over her shoulder and whinnied until K. followed her.

"She's teaching K. to turn left," whispered Elmer.

"Yes," Einer whispered back.

Elmer climbed down and turned Kristie around as they always did. He turned Kristie around so that she could turn left again on the road to the lake. Kristie whinnied and Little K. followed after her.

"Do you think that Kristie is getting to like her?" whispered Elmer.

"S-s-sh! She might hear you. It might be that," whispered Einer.

On they went until they were half way to the lake. Then Kristie stopped.

"Gid-ap," said Elmer.

"We're not there yet," said Einer. "Gid-ap."

But Kristie did not move.

"What's the matter now?" asked Elmer.

"Where's Little K.?" asked Einer.

They looked back along the road. Kristie looked back too.

"There she is lying down in the grass," said Elmer.

"She's so tired," said Einer.

Kristie whinnied as loud as she could. She whinnied so loud that Elmer and Einer jumped on the seat. Little K. stumbled to her feet. She came wobbling down the road on her legs that were so long.

"Poor thing," said Elmer. "She's too tired to walk."

"Yes," said Einer. "Let's put her in the back of the wagon." Elmer and Einer climbed out of the buggy and lifted Little K. in their arms. They lifted her up and put her in the box at the back.

"There," said Elmer, "go to sleep."

"Go to sleep and take a rest," said Einer.

They climbed up to the seat of the buggy. Elmer drove and Einer leaned over the back of the seat to be sure that Little K. did not fall out. Good Old Kristie kept looking over her shoulder and rolling her eyes to see that Little K. was still there.

At last they came to the lake. They lifted Little K. from the buggy and unhitched Kristie.

Elmer and Einer were grinning and grinning. Their grins were twice too wide for their faces. They grinned all the time they were swimming. There were Kristie and Little K. standing close together. There they stood trying to eat the same blade of grass!

"I do believe she likes her," said Elmer.

[32]

"I do believe she does."

"Yes," Einer said. "It's plain to see that at last Good Old Kristie likes Little K. She won't go without her."

Elmer and Einer grinned and grinned and they lived happily ever after with their good horse, Kristie, and Little K.

CAKE

FOR KATIE

Once upon a time, on a farm in Dakota County, there lived a farmer and his wife. And what did they have but a granddaughter, Katie.

The farmer was thin and his wife was thinner. But that Katie was plump as the plumpest grandchild that ever was, and that was plump indeed. She had two round eyes, a round nose and a rounder mouth in her big, round face.

Now Katie liked to eat. Yes, that she did. She liked to eat better than anything else. She liked oatmeal and milk and prunes and even carrots. But what Katie liked best of all was— well, that was cake. Cake! Round cakes, or even square cakes or long cakes or thin cakes, or even thick cakes. But cake it was that Katie liked best.

One day Katie had a birthday as all good children do every so often. It was the eighth birthday that Katie had had in all her eight years.

It was a pretty morning. The sun was shining, the birds were singing and Katie was brushing her teeth. The farmer's wife was smiling and humming to herself. She knew what she was giving Katie for her birthday. She knew very well. But the farmer did not know. And his granddaughter Katie did not know. They could not even guess.

The farmer's wife was humming "Ma-cushla," to herself.

"Are you leaving right away for town, you and Katie?" she asked.

"Yes, right now," answered the farmer, "to buy my present for Katie."

"Oh, goodie," said Katie.

So they went hand in hand out to the car and climbed in. *Chug, chug, wheeze,* they drove off to town.

The farmer's wife at once began to be very busy. She tied the strings of her checkered apron. She rolled up her sleeves.

"I must hurry," said she, "to have it ready when they come back."

She built a fire in the stove, a fire of corn-cobs and wood. She took a huge yellow bowl from the cupboard. It had three blue stripes running all around it. She tucked it in the crook of her left arm, and in her right hand

she took a big wooden spoon. That she did.

With fast long steps she went out of the kitchen and crossed the yard over to the milk house under the maple tree. She was humming to herself: "Macushla, macushla."

"Mew, mew," said the white cat, rubbing his back against her legs.

"What, are you hungry again?"

"Mew," said the cat.

She went into the milk house. The walls were clean with whitewash. There were crocks of butter on the shelf, cans of milk in a tank of cool water.

The farmer's wife took a paddleful of butter from a crock and put it in the bowl.

"Mew," said the cat.

"Oh, all right," said the farmer's wife. She dipped a dipperful of milk into the cat's bowl by the door.

"There you are, greedy puss."

With fast long steps she crossed the farmyard. She beat and stirred the butter in the big yellow bowl as she walked. That she did. *Spat, spat, stir,* to make the butter creamy. *Spat, spat, stir.*

With quick long steps she crossed the farmyard to the red granary. Inside were the bins of oats and bran, the sacks of chicken feed, and the bundles of straw, the charcoal, and the oyster shell. Near the door sat a barrel of flour and a barrel of sugar.

The farmer's wife took off the cover of the sugar barrel and scooped a scoopful of sugar into the bowl with the butter.

"Quack, quack, honk," said the ducks and the geese.

They were poking their yellow bills in at the door of the granary. Two white geese and a gander and three fat, gray ducks.

"Quack, honk, honk!"

[39]

"Oh, all right," said the farmer's wife and she threw a cupful of oats at them. "Here you are, greedy birds," she said.

With long, fast steps she crossed the farm-yard. *Stir, crunch, pat,* she stirred the sugar into the butter. *Stir, crunch, pat,* until it was all smooth and sweet in the yellow bowl.

"Macushla, macushla," she was humming to herself.

With fast, long steps she crossed to the pig shelter made of wire and straw.

"Oink, oink," said the pigs.

In the straw walls of the pig shelter were the hens' nests. She took out three eggs and put them in her apron pocket.

"Oink, oink!" said the pigs.

They were snuffling around, China pigs, striped and spotted pigs.

"Oink, oink!" they said.

"Oh, all right," said the farmer's wife and

she threw the pigs some corn from a bin.

"There you are, you greedy pigs."

With fast long steps she crossed the farm-yard.

"Cackle, cackle," said the white chickens. "Cackle, cackle!"

"Oh, all right," said the farmer's wife.

Crack! One egg in the bowl and she threw the shell down to the chickens. *Crack!* Two eggs in the bowl and *crack,* three eggs in the bowl and the pieces of shell on the ground for the chickens.

"There you are, greedy chicks," she said.

She stirred the eggs in the bowl. *Slop, stir. Slop, stir,* all golden yellow. *Slop, slop, stir,* in her yellow bowl.

She came again to the milk house under the maple tree and went in. She dipped a dipper of milk into the bowl and began to stir. *Gurgle, slop, stir.* The white milk beat round

and round in the yellow bowl. She held the bowl level in her arm as she walked along and did not spill a drop. That she did not. *Gurgle, slop, stir!*

The robins flew over to see whether there was anything to eat and the sparrows chattered in the maple tree. The bees took a smell, *buzz, buzz.*

"Macushla, macushla," the farmer's wife was humming to herself.

Gurgle, slop, stir. She did not spill a drop.

With long fast steps she crossed to the red granary and in at the door. She took the cover from the flour barrel and shook two scoops of flour into the big bowl. And she began to *stir, puff, flop, stir. Puff, flop, stir,* in her yellow bowl.

With quick long steps she crossed the farmyard, *puff, flop, stir.*

"Mew," said the cat, and ran after her.

[43]

"Quack, quack, honk," said the ducks and the geese.

And the cat and the two geese and the gander and the three fat gray ducks followed after her. And the chickens squawked and ran after her too. And the pigs came too and followed. That they did.

"Mew, honk, quack, quack, oink, cackle, cackle!" they all said as they ran after the farmer's wife.

"No more food," she said, "you greedy things!"

Stir, flop, stir. She took fast long steps over to the kitchen door and left them all outside.

The wood in the stove was crackling and the oven was hot.

"Macushla, macushla," she was humming to herself.

With long fast steps she went into the pantry. She stirred in the baking powder and the salt and the nutmeg and a little cinnamon and the vanilla. Stir, round and round in the yellow bowl. And the cake was ready, smooth, light, fluffy in the yellow bowl. She poured it into a big round pan and popped it into the oven.

"There," said she, looking at the kitchen clock. "It will be done by dinner time."

And when Katie and her grandfather came back from town, the cake was all baked. And there was chocolate icing on it and eight yellow candles and another one to grow on.

Katie put on her new red dress that her grandfather had bought for her. It was fat enough even for Katie. And she tied her new red ribbons on her black hair. Her eyes were rounder and bluer than ever.

And that was a birthday party if there ever was one.

"Oh, the cake is so good!" said Katie.

And that it was. It was sweet and spicy and melted in her mouth. Such cake no one ever ate before nor after.

And Katie—Katie—well, Katie ate—Katie ate—more than one piece!

That she did!

PEDER'S GULL

Once upon a time, a year or so ago, there lived on the North Shore of Lake Superior, a little boy named Peder. He lived there with his mother and his father and his little sister, Birgit. His Grandfather Gunderson lived there too.

"Would anyone like a picnic?" asked Grandfather Gunderson one day in June.

"Oh, yes," shouted Peder and Birgit in one loud shout. "Oh, yes. When can we start?"

"I'll fix the boat while you put up the lunch," their grandfather answered.

So Birgit made some cheese sandwiches, and Peder counted out plenty of doughnuts. They put them in the picnic basket and filled in the chinks with cherries.

"We're ready," shouted Peder and Birgit.

"All right. Yust hop in," said Grandfather Gunderson.

And in a moment he was rowing the white fishing skiff out of the cove. It skimmed over the smooth water of the lake.

"Where shall it be?" he asked.

"Gull Island," said Peder.

"Yes, Gull Island," said Birgit. "The baby gulls will be out. We saw the eggs last time we were there."

Grandfather Gunderson rowed along the shore and then out to Gull Island. The gulls were flying in huge circles over the rocks. They were swooping and drifting over the rocks and screaming all the time.

"What a terrible noise," said Birgit.

"They're afraid we'll hurt their children," said Peder, "but of course we wouldn't."

"Don't be afraid," said Birgit to the gulls.

But the gulls kept right on with their flying and their scolding.

"Come over to the woody part of the island," said Grandfather Gunderson. "Then they'll not be afraid."

They sat down on the soft moss under some balsam firs.

"Isn't it time to eat right away?" asked Peder.

Grandfather looked at the sun.

"Well, it's yust noon exactly," he said.

"Oh, then we must eat," said Peder.

Birgit uncovered the lunch basket and gave them each a sandwich. And before you could ever imagine that it could have happened, all the food was gone. All the sand-

[49]

wiches and all the doughnuts and all the cherries were eaten up.

"Now let's look at the babies," said Birgit.

She and Peder crept slowly out of the woods to the rocks.

"There are some out there," whispered Peder.

"Aren't they cute!" said Birgit softly.

The little brown gulls were sitting beside their big white mothers. One of the mothers was squawking and trying to push her children into the water. One little gull would not move but sat there squeaking in a shrill voice.

"That one is naughty," said Birgit. "It does not want to take a bath."

"I think it is hurt," said Peder. "Oh, look! Its foot is caught. It is caught between two rocks. Grandfather," he called.

Grandfather Gunderson came hurrying toward them.

"What can the matter be?" he asked.

"It's that baby gull. Its foot is caught," said Peder.

"You stay here and I'll see," said Grandfather.

He walked slowly out to the rocks. The gulls beat their wings and shrieked. They almost flew in his face. The mothers all hurried their babies into the water and swam away with them. Grandfather Gunderson stooped down over the little gull. He pulled the foot gently this way and that until it was free.

"The leg is broken," he called to Peder and Birgit. "I'll fetch it along and bind it up."

He carried the little gull carefully in his big hands. It was too frightened at first to squeak. Then it cuddled down and kept very still.

"We'll put it in the basket and take it home."

[51]

They climbed into the fishing skiff and Peder held the basket carefully on his knees. The gulls were still circling overhead and shrieking.

"Don't be afraid," Birgit said to the gulls. "We're just going to fix its leg. We won't hurt it."

As soon as they reached home, Grandfather Gunderson took a little stick and bound it tightly to the leg. The gull looked so funny standing on one foot. It stood there opening its mouth and squealing.

"It's hungry," said Grandfather, "and now you must feed it, Peder."

"Bread and milk?" asked Birgit.

"Fish," said Peder.

"Yes, fish," said Grandfather Gunderson. "There are those fine fish I brought in this morning."

So Peder gave some fish to the gull and it

stopped crying. They fixed a soft nest of straw for it and it went to sleep.

Every day Peder fed the gull. A dozen times a day he fed it. And every day the gull grew larger. It was very fond of Peder and flapped its wings and squeaked whenever he came near. It liked Birgit too, but she was afraid to feed it. It might gobble up her fingers along with the fish, she thought.

The gull would fly above the rocks of the cove. Sometimes it rested on the quiet water. Or it spread its wings and drifted before the wind on stormy days. It grew larger and larger and could catch its own food before long. One day Grandfather Gunderson took the splint from the broken leg.

"It must be knit by now," he said. "The leg is yust a little crooked, but it will do to stand on."

"See! It's using it all right," cried Peder. "It works."

The gull looked its leg over carefully and then stepped off over the rock.

"It is very proud," said Peder.

"It does work all right," said Grandfather Gunderson. He was proud too.

The gull grew bigger and bigger until it was as large as the older gulls. It was very fond of Peder. It would pick up Peder's ball, fly around in big circles and drop it again on the rocks. One day it carried the ball far out over the lake and came back without it.

"Well, that good ball is rolling on the water somewhere," said Peder.

One day the gull flew off with Peder's cap and came back without it.

"Well, that good cap is floating on the lake somewhere," said Peder.

Every day flocks of screaming gulls came in from the lake to eat the fish heads that Grandfather threw out for them. "Gulls are the fisherman's friend," Grandfather always said. There were the older white gulls and the young brown ones. Peder's gull would fly around with them. It looked like any one of the brown ones. Peder could not tell which it was. But when the gulls flew away, it always came circling back and sat on Peder's rock.

"It certainly knows its home," Peder said.

"You've been a good mamma to it," said Birgit.

"Mamma!" said Peder. "Father, you mean."

"Anyway, he's fed and played with it," said Grandfather Gunderson. "This is its home."

But one day late in summer Peder's gull flew away. It flew away with the white and brown gulls that came to eat Grandfather Gunderson's fish heads. And Peder's gull flew away with them.

"It'll come back," Peder said. "It always comes back."

But the gull did not come back.

Peder stood out on the rocks and called. His grandfather rowed him out on the lake and Peder called. He called to all the brown gulls he saw. But none of them came back.

"Well, it's nature," said Grandfather Gunderson. "After all, it's yust nature, Peder. The gull was tame, but it's really a wild thing, you know. It would fly off with the others some-time, Peder."

Peder held his lips tight together to keep from crying.

"You can have my tapioca pudding to-night, Peder," said Birgit. "Two dishes might make you feel better."

Peder smiled faintly.

"You know," he said, "I was v-v-very f-f-fond of that gull. I really was."

Every day Peder watched for the gull. Fall came and winter, but the gull did not come back.

"The worst of it is I'd never know it now, because it would be white. It would have shed its baby feathers and be white like all the oth-ers by this time."

"It's nature, Peder," said his grandfather. "Ya, it's happy with the wild birds. It was happy with you too, Peder, but not for always."

"Now that it is grown up," said Peder, "it is better with the wild ones."

"But it might come back for a visit some day," said Birgit.

And perhaps it did come back. For the next spring whenever the gulls flew in to gobble up Grandfather's fish heads, one of the gulls would stay behind for a while. It was a beautiful white gull. It seemed to be more beautiful than the others, Peder thought. It would fly in wide circles and sit on Peder's rocks.

"Is that you?" Peder called. "Are you my gull?"

But the gull would fly off over the lake again.

Once Peder thought he saw a crooked leg. Once the gull flew in alone and sat around on

the rocks all day. It seemed to feel at home there. One day it walked along the rocks close to the rock where Peder was sitting.

"Are you my gull?" asked Peder softly.

Then one day the gull snatched up Peder's new cap and flew away with it.

"Oh, that *is* my gull!" shouted Peder. "That *is* my gull, as sure as anything!"

"Ya, maybe so," said Grandfather Gunderson. "Maybe so. It might be now. It might remember us."

"It must be my gull!" cried Peder, his blue eyes shining. "Going off with my cap that way. It must be! What fun to have it coming back again!"

"On visits," said Birgit. "What fun!"

"My own gull!" said Peder. "It *does* remember me!"

HELPING
HILDA

Hilda was the most helping child on the banks of the Father of Waters. She began helping when she slid from her bed in the morning. She helped all through the livelong day and stopped only when she climbed into bed at night.

She helped her mother and her father in their home in the city. Now that she was visiting Aunt Selma in Little River, she was helping her.

She could make beds without losing the blankets on the floor more than once or twice.

She could dust the chairs and the tables and leave most of the vases on the bookcases. She wiped only a few handles from the cups and she could carry a bag of groceries along the village street without spilling more than one or two things. She was a great help to everyone.

"Are you coming with me to buy the groceries, Hilda?" Aunt Selma asked one day. "When we come back I will make gingerbread."

"Oh, goodie!" shouted Hilda. "Gingerbread! I like that just about more than chocolate cake. Can I help make it?"

"Why, yes," said Aunt Selma. "There are some things you could do to help."

Hilda had an idea.

"I think I will stay at home and do the dusting. Then I'll be ready to help with the gingerbread."

Aunt Selma looked a little surprised, because Hilda liked to go shopping better than anything else.

"Oh, all right, Hilda. There will not be much to carry home. I can easily do it," and Aunt Selma with her bag over her arm walked away toward Main Street where the grocery was.

Hilda danced a jig in the middle of the living room and tossed her dusting mitt in the air.

"I'll just hurry and finish this and then—"

She swished here and she swushed there. A book fell on the floor, but the vases only rocked around some. Swish, swush. All the time she was singing under her breath: "Gingerbread, gingerbread, molasses and brown sugar, eggs and milk and flour and eggs and sugar, molasses and ginger, ginger, ginger! Oh, yum, yum, yum!"

"There, that will do," sang Hilda, as she

tossed the dusting mitt into the closet and skipped into the kitchen.

She tied on Aunt Selma's apron that came down to her feet.

"I will just get out all the things to make the gingerbread. What a help it will be!"

"Milk," said Hilda.

She carried the milk from the refrigerator.

"Lard," said Hilda. "Butter, maybe," and she put them on the table.

"Ginger."

She opened the can of ginger and sniffed a hard sniff, such a hard sniff that her nose tickled.

"Eggs next," she said.

She took out some eggs and held them in her hands. She held them in her hands while she wriggled her nose all around and up and down to keep from sneezing. It was the ginger sneeze.

"Atch, atch, atch," cried Hilda. "Atch, atch, atch, CHEW!"

The sneeze shook Hilda all over. It shook her head. It twitched her hair. It shook her shoulders and her arms. It twitched her hands. And away flew one of the eggs. Sklutch! Down on the floor!

[65]

"Oh, dear," said Hilda. "It broke. It broke all in pieces. I'll have to pick it up."

Hilda put the other eggs carefully on the table and bent over. It was easy to pick up the shell, but the lump of white and yellow slid away. She tried to scoop it up with a spoon. The egg slipped this way and that. Her fingers could not push it into the spoon.

Slowly Hilda backed away as the egg slid over the floor. Hilda backed and the egg slid after her. It slid from the refrigerator to the table to the sink and to the back door. It left a long slippery streak behind it. It grew smaller and smaller until there was only a little blob of it left.

Hilda looked at it and sighed.

"Guess I'll just have to scrub the floor."

And she did. She sloshed it, and she scrubbed it, and she wiped it. She scrubbed until the egg was all washed away.

[66]

"There. That will help Aunt Selma," said
Hilda, as she wrung out the scrubbing rag and
pushed some wet hair back from her forehead.
"She won't have to scrub the floor. Now the
molasses."

Hilda carried the molasses bottle to the
table and tried to turn the top. She jerked and
twisted.

"It's stuck!"

Just then Nils Nilsson came across the kitchen. He was Aunt Selma's white cat. Nils Nilsson mewed and rubbed against Hilda's legs.

She jerked at the bottle top. She jerked and twisted. And flip! Off the top came. The bottle rocked on the table. It tipped over and the molasses began to run. A thick sticky stream ran over the table and down on the floor. It ran over Nils Nilsson's feet, the sticky brown molasses.

Nils Nilsson did not like molasses. He did not like it to eat and he liked it even less on his feet. He jumped high in the air and then skipped across the kitchen. He climbed up the kitchen curtains and down again. Then he hid behind the stove.

Hilda stood with her hands in the air as the drops of molasses flew from the feet of Nils Nilsson all over and up and down. All around on the floor, all over the curtains, all over the stove!

[68]

"Nils!" she cried. "Why, Nils, Nils! There is molasses on everything. Come let me wash you, before you do any more."

She pulled Nils from under the stove and carried him to the sink. She scrubbed his feet with the scrubbing rag as well as she could. Nils wriggled so fast that she was not sure which foot she had just washed, but she did eight of them as well as she could. Then she put him out the back door.

"I think I had better scrub the floor again."

And she did. She scrubbed up all the sticky spots that she could find. She washed the bottoms of her shoes and the top of the table. She wiped the molasses bottle all around.

"I'll have to wash the curtains too, I guess, and Aunt Selma's apron," and she put them to soak in a pan of water. "Aunt Selma will be glad to have this done for her. The curtains and the apron will be clean. Perhaps I could iron them too. Where did the top of the molasses bottle go?"

"Hello there," and in walked Aunt Selma back from her marketing. "Oh, you've been helping!"

"Yes," and Hilda crawled out from under the sink with the top of the molasses bottle clutched in her hand. Her face was red. There

was a streak of molasses across her chin.

"Yes," she said, as she wiped the bottle top with the scrubbing rag. "I've been getting things ready for the gingerbread. And cleaning up a little too. The egg and the molasses, you know. I've scrubbed Nils and the kitchen floor, two times I scrubbed the floor. Perhaps you had better iron the curtains, because my ironing is wobbly, but I did the rest. Aren't I a big help to you, Aunt Selma?"

Aunt Selma was very busy getting out the gingerbread recipe.

"Oh, Hilda," she cried and she was laughing. "You are the most helpingest girl in this whole wide country. I don't know what I would do without you!"

Hilda was pulling her foot from a sticky place on the floor.

"Now what more can I do to help?" she asked.

TAKING
CARE OF
NELLIE

Steve and Nancy lived in a little town on the banks of a big river. Their father was Mr. Barker. He was a plump and pleasant man with blue eyes that always looked a little surprised. He worked in an old-and-new furniture store on Main Street and did not have much money. He had only enough to buy clothing and food for the four of them and there was not a penny left over for fancies.

Mrs. Barker was pleasant too and very

plump and a little more surprised than Mr. Barker. She was surprised when the bread was all eaten and when holes came in the toes of socks and in the elbows of shirts and dresses. But she always knew what to do when they did. She just baked more bread and darned the holes and patched the elbows and kept the family as fat and neat as she possibly could. But sometimes she wished they had a little more money for some fancies for the children.

And of course Steve and Nancy were plump too and they would have liked some fancies. But they had never been able to make up their minds as to what the fancy would be if they ever had enough money to buy one.

One day Mr. Barker came home all smiling with excitement. His blue eyes were bigger than ever. He took off his coat, rolled up his sleeves and put on his overalls.

[73]

"Where's your oldest broom?" he asked Mrs. Barker.

"Whatever are you going to do?" she asked.

"Get ready for a boarder," he answered.

"A boarder?" said Mrs. Barker. "But all the rooms are filled with just the family! Where could we put a boarder?"

"In the barn," said Mr. Barker. He was grinning and chuckling to himself.

"Whoever heard of such a thing!" cried Mrs. Barker, looking so surprised that her eyes were twice their size. "A boarder in a barn!"

Steve and Nancy were standing with their mouths open, listening.

"Is it a horse, Dad?" asked Steve.

"Oh, is it?" cried Nancy.

"Of course," said their father. "Bill O'Brien wants a place to board his horse for the winter and I said I would do it for fifteen dollars. We have the barn and a stall and everything. Need a little food. That's all. See, here's the money."

Mr. Barker pulled out his pocketbook and there it was, ten worn and wrinkled bills, a five and nine ones and the rest in clinking change.

"Oh, Dad!" said Steve and Nancy. They had never seen so much money before.

"Come on," said their father. "We must get the barn ready for Nellie. Bill's bringing her over tonight."

Mr. Barker hurried to the barn and began sweeping as fast as he could. The dust puffed out at the doorway. He swept the stall all up and down and he swept the floor. Mrs. Barker brought a pail of water, soap, and a brush and scrubbed the stall from top to bottom. Steve dusted the little old black car that they kept

[75]

in the barn and used only on Sundays and holidays. Nancy washed the barn windows until they shone.

"There, that's clean," said Mr. Barker, as the family looked proudly around, their faces pinker than ever from their hard work. "Now Steve and Nancy can take care of Nellie and earn some money for fancies."

Steve and Nancy were still smiling widely when Nellie herself came with Bill O'Brien and a wagon of straw and feed. And they were smiling more widely when Bill went back home and left Nellie with them.

Nellie was a very friendly horse and leaned up against Steve and Nancy when they patted her neck. She was too thin and showed more ribs than a horse really should show. The plump and pleasant Barkers felt sorry for her.

"She should be fatter," said Mr. Barker, as he bounced his fingers over her ribs.

"We'll feed her up well," said the children.

"Yes, we must show that we are good people to take care of a horse," said Mrs. Barker.

So they spread straw on the stall floor for a bed and put oats in the feed box. Mr. Barker unharnessed Nellie and led her in at the door. She blew big breaths out of her nostrils to be sure that everything was all right. Her new home must have pleased her, because she began to eat her oats as if she had always lived there.

And that was only the beginning of a busy winter for the Barkers. They took very good care of Nellie. They did it so well that it took all of their time that was not already filled with everyday things like working in the store for Mr. Barker, going to school for Steve and Nancy, and making bread and darning holes for their mother.

They gave her just so much oats and just so much hay and a little bran. Sometimes they mixed egg with the oats because that would make her coat shine.

If there were not many eggs in the house, Steve would say: "We don't really need eggs

for breakfast today, but Nellie does."

They brushed Nellie and curried her and even scrubbed her with kills-all-odor soap to be sure that she was clean. And Nellie was about the cleanest horse that ever went around on four legs. She grew fatter, too, until her ribs were neatly out of sight and her sides shone as if they were varnished.

And Nellie was happy too. She was even more happy when Mr. Barker gave her the sugar that he saved from his breakfast coffee.

Every day after school, Steve and Nancy took Nellie out for exercise, leading her down to the pond for a drink. They hitched her to the old wagon and drove her out of town along the country roads. Taking care of a horse boarder was so much fun—and then there was the money they would have for fancies. There was all the money that would be left from the fifteen dollars when Nellie went back home in the spring.

Mrs. Barker had hidden the money away in a box behind the top row of books in the bookcase on the left-hand side. Whenever they bought oats or straw for Nellie, they took out a bill or two and put the change back in the box.

"What shall we buy?" said Steve. "What fancy shall we bring?"

"Something for all of us," said Nancy. "Whatever can it be? What fancy could we buy?"

The cold snappy days of fall grew snappier. The red line in the thermometer went lower. It was winter. The snow fell and the wind blew. It was that cold wind that began to bring wrinkles to the brows of the plump and pleasant Barkers. The winter wind whistled through the cracks of the old barn and blew around the corners and into Nellie's stall. It was very cold.

"This will never do," said Mr. Barker. "We can't have Nellie catching cold."

But Mrs. Barker knew what to do with wind blowing in cracks. She was used to being surprised by things like that, elbows bursting out of sleeves and toes popping out of stockings.

"We must fill up the cracks," she said. "We must stuff the cracks with rags and newspapers."

And that is what the Barkers did. They pushed rags and pieces of newspaper into as many of the cracks as they could. They packed them in hard, but still the wind blew in.

"We can't stuff all the cracks," said Mr. Barker. "There are just too many of them."

Steve and Nancy felt unhappy, but Mrs. Barker knew what to do.

[81]

"There are some old quilts up in the attic that I have been saving for something. We can hang them around the stall."

The family climbed up to the attic and carried down three quilts and an old blanket. One, a red quilt, they hung in the doorway of the stall. The others, patchwork quilts, they hung over the stall like a tent to keep the wind from blowing down Nellie's neck. Over her back they put the blanket. Nellie looked like a circus horse all ready for the ring.

"Now, she'll surely be warm enough," said Mr. Barker.

"Oh, yes," said the children.

Nellie whinnied a soft warm whinny.

Mrs. Barker looked all around to be sure that everything was snug and tight. That was the way she looked over a darn to be sure she had filled it all in.

"Yes, now she will be warm enough," she

said, and all the plump and pleasant Barkers went into the house and warmed their cold fingers over the kitchen stove.

But the winter grew more wintry still. The red in the thermometer grew shorter. It went down to zero. The Barkers gave Nellie more oats to make her fatter and drove her along the snowy roads to keep her well. They combed her and brushed her and put more straw under her feet to keep them warm. But the red in the thermometer went lower and lower. It was so short that you could hardly find it. Twenty below! The barn was colder than the North Pole.

The Barkers stood in front of the stall stamping to warm their feet. Their breath curled out from their mouths like smoke. And Nellie's breath looked like a volcano.

"What can we do?" they cried.

"Take her into the house," said Steve.

[83]

"She can have my room," said Nancy.

"Oh, I could never have a horse in the house! I really couldn't," cried Mrs. Barker. "And how would she get upstairs?"

"There's just one thing," said Mr. Barker who knew all about furniture and things because he worked in an old-and-new furniture store. "We'll have to buy a stove."

"Of course," said all the family.

"We'll buy an airtight stove," he said, "and some corncobs to burn in it."

"Of course," they all cried.

And that is what the Barkers did. They took some money from the box hidden in the bookcase and bought an airtight stove and a wagonload of corncobs. Nellie herself fetched them in her old wagon. Mr. Barker set up the airtight stove with the stovepipe sticking out through the side of the barn. The stove was near Nellie's stall and soon the cobs were

burning hotly in it. Nellie's home was as warm
and beautiful as a prince's palace.

The family stood around the stove and
smiled proudly.

"Now she'll be warm enough," they said
to each other.

Nellie was warm enough and had all she could eat. She had treats of sugar and sometimes apples. She was so clean that her coat shone and she exercised enough to keep from getting too fat. She was the happiest horse in all the country round and the Barkers were happy with her.

January passed and February too. The days grew longer. March came and the snow began to thaw. April came, and rain and green grass and flowers. The winter was over and spring was here. It was time for Bill O'Brien to take Nellie home again.

And he came one morning and drove Nellie away with her old wagon. He thought the Barkers had done a very good job in caring for Nellie. He scarcely knew her for his horse, she was so beautiful.

The Barkers were lonesome with Nellie gone and they had so much time for everything. Mr. Barker dawdled about planting his garden and Mrs. Barker strolled up and down doing her spring cleaning. And Steve and Nancy slowly did their lessons and then sat out in the barn and wished that Nellie were back again.

And what about the box of board money hidden away in the bookcase behind the top row of books on the left-hand side? After Nellie went, the family took out the box and counted the money and they tried to be happy about it. There really was very little to be happy about. They had taken such good care of Nellie and bought her so much oats and hay and straw, and a stove to keep her warm and corncobs to burn in it. They had taken such good care of her, that in the box hidden in the bookcase there was only one dime, one nickel and two pennies. Just seventeen cents! Not a penny more!

"Seventeen cents for a fancy," said Steve. "Whatever can we buy for seventeen cents?"

"Something to eat?" asked Nancy. "Let's see, whatever can it be for seventeen cents for all of us? What can it be?"

"Four cents each and a penny over," said Mr. Barker who knew about money and things because he worked in an old-and-new furniture store.

"Whatever can it be?" asked Mrs. Barker. Whatever could it be for seventeen cents? Do you know?

A NOTE ON THE TYPE

The text of this book was set on the Linotype in Baskerville, a facsimile of the type designed by John Baskerville, Birmingham, England, in 1754. The original Baskerville type was one of the forerunners of the "modern" style of type faces. The Linotype copy was cut under the supervision of George W. Jones of London.

The book was composed by *H. Wolff*, New York. Printed and bound by The Book Press, Brattleboro, Vermont.